Clangers

LOOKiNG FOR A LULLABY

GROSSET & DUNLAP
AN IMPRINT OF
PENGUIN RANDOM HOUSE

GROSSET & DUNLAP
PENGUIN YOUNG READERS GROUP
AN IMPRINT OF PENGUIN RANDOM HOUSE LLC

coolabi

WWW.CLANGERS.COM

COPYRIGHT © 2016 COOLABI PRODUCTIONS LIMITED, SMALLFILMS LIMITED,
AND PETER FIRMIN. ALL RIGHTS RESERVED. PUBLISHED BY GROSSET & DUNLAP,
AN IMPRINT OF PENGUIN RANDOM HOUSE LLC, 345 HUDSON STREET,
NEW YORK, NEW YORK 10014. GROSSET & DUNLAP IS A TRADEMARK OF
PENGUIN RANDOM HOUSE LLC. MANUFACTURED IN CHINA.

ISBN 978-0-399-54144-5   10 9 8 7 6 5 4 3 2 1

On a faraway planet, deep in space, Tiny times a perfect catch.

As Small races around the bases, she throws to home . . .

CLANG!

The home plate lid flies open,
and Mother Clanger snatches the ball.

"Bedtime!" she announces firmly.

Sadly, Small and Tiny wave
good-bye to their friends.

They'll have to finish
the Clangerball
game in their dreams.

Down below, everyone
shares a family hug
before calling good night
to one another from
their bed caves.

Tiny dons her radio hat and makes her nightly bedtime call to Iron Chicken.

From her nest high above the planet, Iron Chicken tunes in. "Hello, Tiny Clanger. Are you ready for your lullaby?"

"Yes, please!" replies Tiny. She hugs Sky Moo and snuggles down as Iron Chicken warms up her voice.

"DO-RE-MI-FA-
SOL-LA-TI-SQUAWK-
DO-DO-DO!"

Then, Iron Chicken clucks, clangs, and croons:

"GO TO SLEEP, MY TINY, CLOSE YOUR LITTLE EYES.
GO TO SLEEP, MY TINY, TILL MORNING WHEN YOU RISE . . ."

Suddenly, the melody changes:

"GO TO SLEE"—SCREE—SCREECH!
WHIRR—"EEEE"—"TINY"—
TINNY—WHREEETCHH!

What is wrong with the radio hat?! Tiny shakes it and tries again.

WWHiR! SCREEE! SCREEEECH!!!

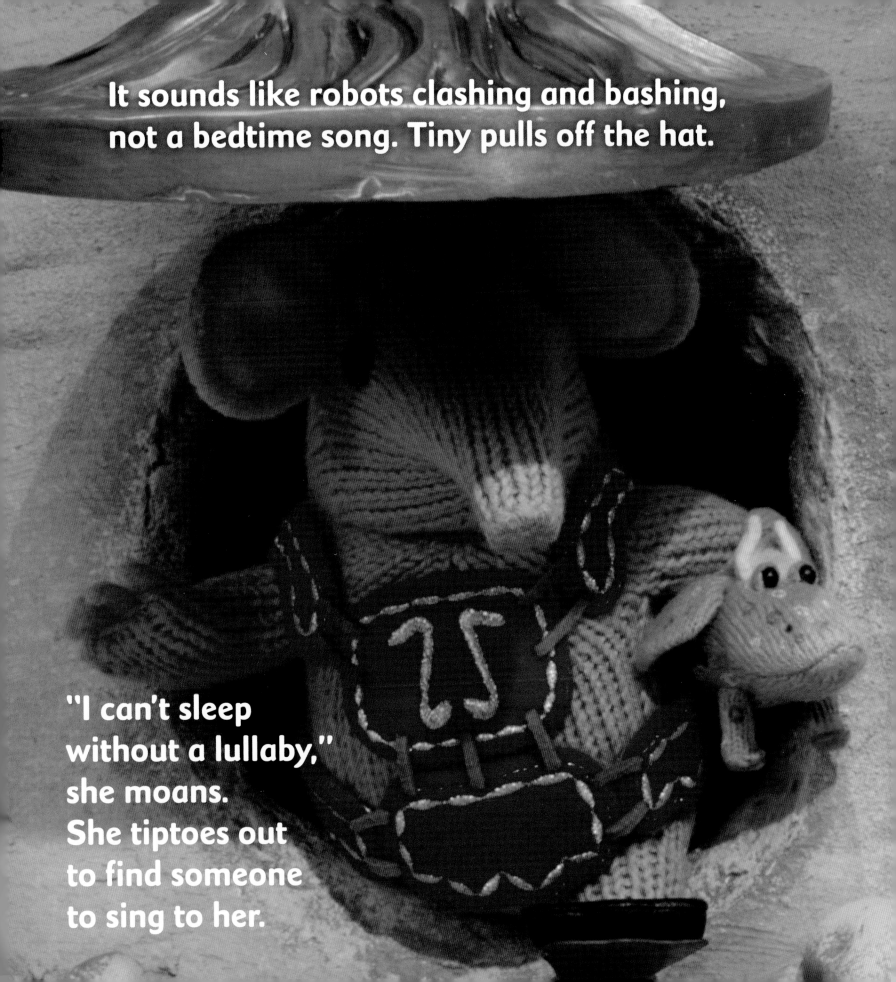

It sounds like robots clashing and bashing, not a bedtime song. Tiny pulls off the hat.

"I can't sleep without a lullaby," she moans. She tiptoes out to find someone to sing to her.

She places her ear at Granny's door, but Granny is sound asleep.

Tiny pauses by her parents' bed cave. SUH! SNUH! SNNORRRE!

There's a lot of major snoring going on in there!

She finds her flower friends. "Will you sing me a lullaby?" Tiny begs. She keeps her door open to let the flowers' flutey tune float in.

But the song grows louder and wakes Small, who bursts from his bed cave. "What's going on?" he complains, frightening the flowers away.

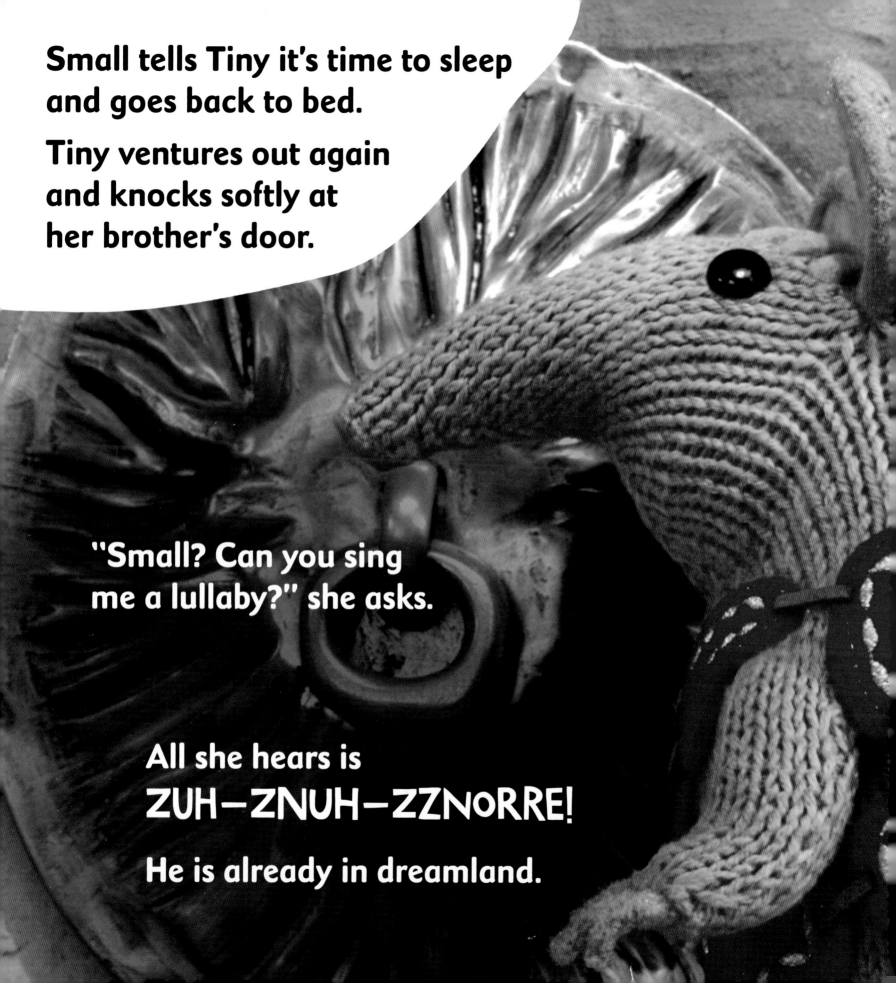

Small tells Tiny it's time to sleep and goes back to bed.

Tiny ventures out again and knocks softly at her brother's door.

"Small? Can you sing me a lullaby?" she asks.

All she hears is ZUH–ZNUH–ZZNoRRE!

He is already in dreamland.

So Tiny tries the Soup Dragon. She lifts a lid and calls down, "Can you sing me a lullaby?"

Soup Dragon pops up. "Shh!" she gently scolds. "You'll wake Baby!"

Next, Tiny pleads with the froglets.
"Do you know any lullabies?"
The froglets think they do. They dip
up and down, beboppin' a crazy tune,
over and over:

"RiBBITTY, RIBBiTT, SLEEPY FoLK,

BOUNCE iN BED, WiG, WAG-CROAK!"

The strong beat shivers and shakes Tiny from her toes to the tip of her nose. She covers her ears and calls out, "Stop, stop, please!"

As Tiny heads
back to her bed
cave, she whispers
sadly to Baby
Soup Dragon,
"I only wanted
a lullaby."

Tiny settles in and sighs. "Good night, Sky Moo." But she hears a loud . . .

KNOCK!
KNOCK!

When Tiny opens up, Baby Soup Dragon asks, "Will you sing a lullaby for me?"

The froglets want to hear one, too.

Tiny shakes her head. "I'm sorry. I can't sing lullabies!"

"Yes, yes, you can!" Baby Soup Dragon tells her.

The froglets join in to make a noisy chorus.

Tiny blinks and thinks. Finally, she invites her friends in and closes the door. She gives Sky Moo to Baby Soup Dragon to cuddle. Then, Tiny takes a deep breath and tries singing softly:

"IT'S TIME FOR BED, TIME FOR BED. TIME FOR BED FOR YOUUU . . ."

Tiny pauses, nods, and finishes:

"TIME FOR BED FOR DRAGONNNS AND FROGLETS AND CLANGERS, TOOO . . ."

Baby Soup Dragon exclaims, "That's a lovely lullaby!"

The froglets bob up and down in agreement.

There's another knock at the door.

Small apologizes for scaring the flowers and asks if he may listen, too.

Tiny hugs her brother. "Of course!" she says.

Her visitors grow cozy
and comfy as Tiny
continues singing sweetly.

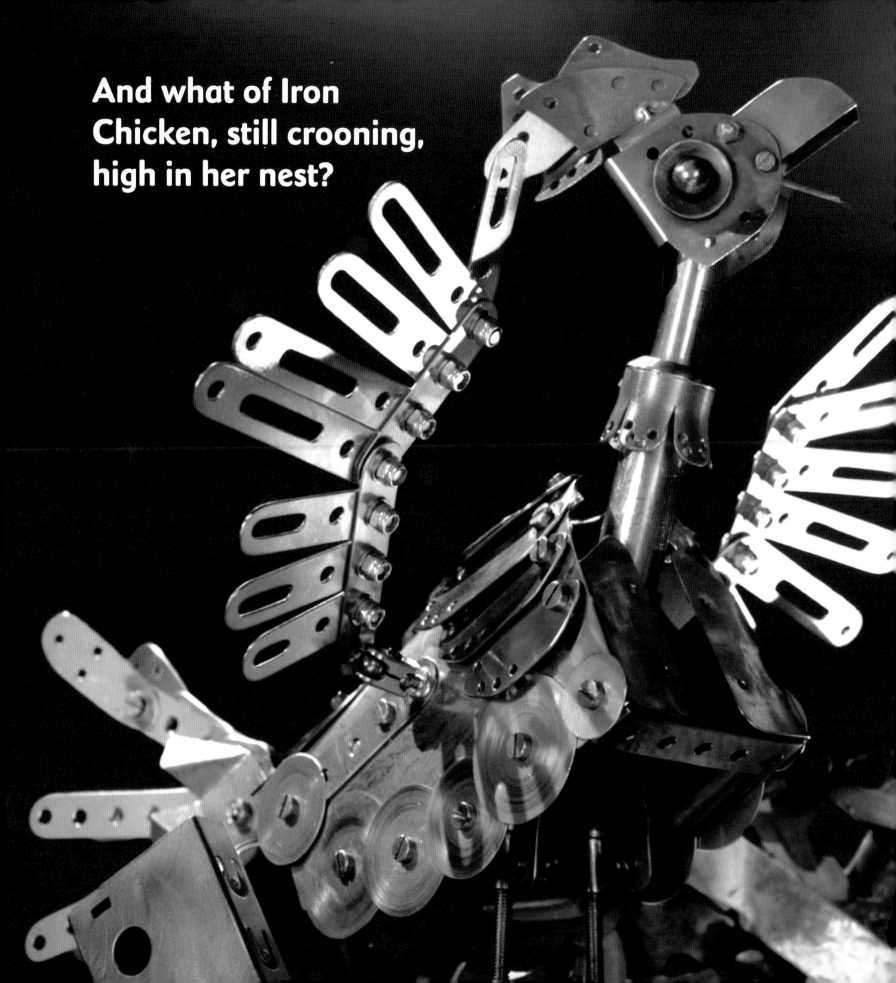

And what of Iron Chicken, still crooning, high in her nest?

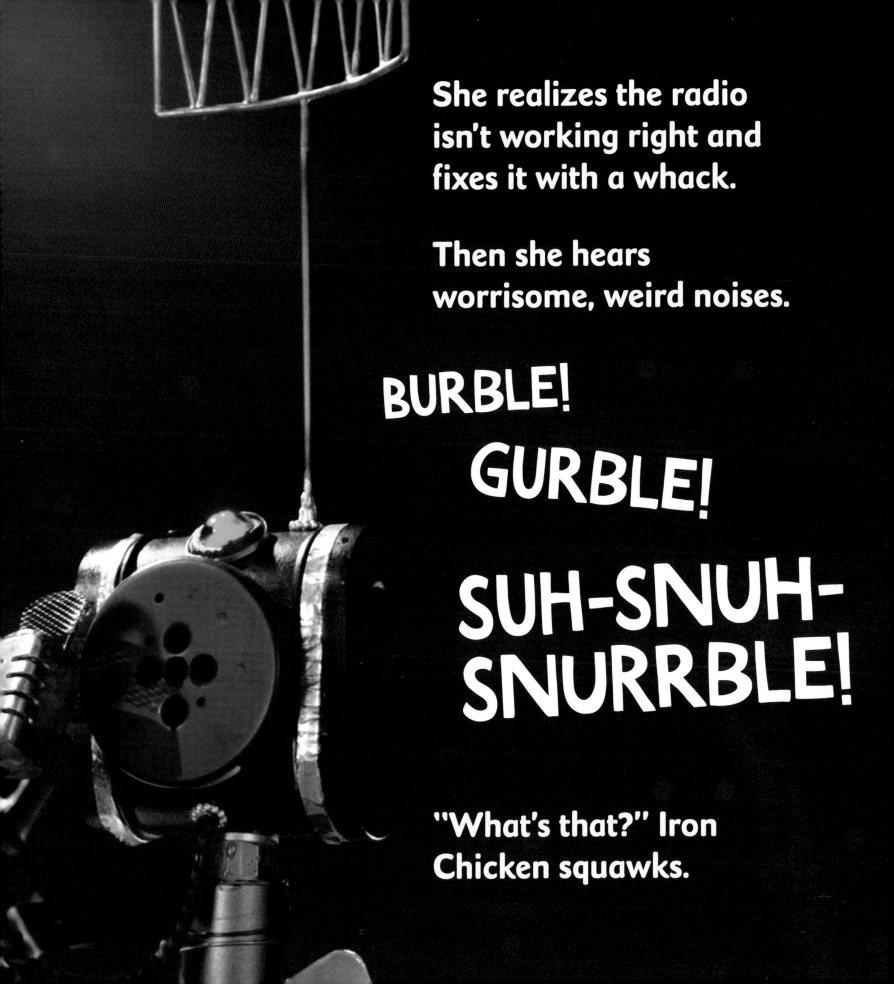

She realizes the radio isn't working right and fixes it with a whack.

Then she hears worrisome, weird noises.

BURBLE!

GURBLE!

SUH-SNUH-SNURRBLE!

"What's that?" Iron Chicken squawks.

She swoops down and tiptoes into Tiny's bed cave to check on things. Everyone is sleeping deeply, and Baby Soup Dragon is snoring like a dinosaur. Ah! Everything is fine. Iron Chicken softly sings and flaps away.

Maybe tomorrow night, Tiny will sing a lullaby with Iron Chicken.